THIS BOOK IS DEDICATED TO LUCA AND WILF

First published in Great Britain in 2013 by Simon and Schuster UK Ltd,
a CBS company.
Simon & Schuster UK Ltd
1st Floor, 222 Gray's Inn Road, London WC1X 8HB

www.simonandschuster.co.uk

Text copyright © Jack Carson 2013
With special thanks to Matt Whyman and Michelle Misra
Cover illustration copyright © Lorenzo Etherington 2013
Interior illustration copyright © Damien Jones 2013

The right of Jack Carson, Lorenzo Etherington and Damien Jones to be identified
as the author and illustrators of this work respectively has been asserted by them
in accordance with sections 77 and 78 of the Copyright,
Designs and Patents Act, 1988.

A CIP catalogue record for this book is available from the British Library.

PB ISBN: 978-0-85707-559-8
eBook ISBN: 978-0-85707-560-4

1 3 5 7 9 10 8 6 4 2

Printed and bound by
CPI Group (UK) Ltd, Croydon, CR0 4YY

THE CHAMPIONSHIP TRAIL

rairie Territory

The Canyon

Mines

Rust Town

dlands

Mines

OCEAN
TERMINAL

Prologue

Sometime in the future, a war destroys the world as we know it. As people struggle to rebuild their lives, a new sport emerges from the ruins. In the Battle Championship, giant robots known as 'mechs' square up to one another and fight like gladiators. They're controlled from the inside by talented pilots, in a fight that tests man and machine to the limit.

All kids grow up dreaming of piloting a mech, and Titch Darwin is no exception. But for Titch it's personal. He is the son of one of the greatest Battle Champions – a man who went missing on the Championship trail – and the only way for Titch to find out what happened is to follow in his father's footsteps . . .

1

Trespassers Must be Punished

Titch Darwin wriggled under the fence surrounding the old air-force base. He wasn't supposed to be here. There would be trouble if he was caught. His eyes narrowed as he looked first one way and then the other. Steel shutters covered the windows of buildings and weeds sprouted up through cracks in the runway. The only planes and helicopters here had been blown up long ago. The whole place looked abandoned, but Titch knew that this wasn't the case. He was looking in at the most famous mech training academy of all.

The sound of thumping metal and clashing chrome filled Titch's ears. It made the ground rumble around him. The noise was coming from a huge hangar on the far side of the airbase. From where he was crouching, he could only see the sidewall. Titch smiled to himself. He was sure that he would find what – or rather who – he was looking for in there. But how could he get across the airstrip without being caught? Guards were standing on watchtowers at every corner of the airbase. Bandits were often drawn to the Academy, hoping to steal a mech and break it down for parts. Titch was short and wiry with a mop of sandy hair that looked like it was charged with static electricity. He could move fast, but this was a dangerous place. If the guards saw Titch, they would assume he was up to no good and throw him out straight away.

Another huge crash from inside the hangar made Titch look over. It was now or never. He couldn't afford to stay out in the open any longer. Up on his feet, Titch dashed across the ground, kicking up dust as he ran. At any moment he expected someone to sound the alarm. All he could do was hope the din coming from the hangar would cover any noise he made.

Breathlessly, Titch reached the side of the great building and pressed his back to the wall. He'd done it! His heart was hammering in his chest when, a moment later, something huge slammed into the other side of the wall. The force of the impact was so great that it caused a dent to punch outwards right beside him. Titch gasped out loud. He was running a huge risk just being here.

'Stay calm,' he muttered to himself. 'There's no going back now.'

Keeping low, but moving swiftly, Titch crept along to the hangar's entrance. Peering round the corner, he gasped at the sight before him — two massive metal machines were squaring up to one another inside.

'Mechs,' he breathed. 'Championship mechs.'

Titch had never seen these fighting machines before with his own eyes. He knew that people flocked to watch the sport. Titch would've loved to have joined them, but he'd always had chores to do for his mother on their cattle ranch. Even though the mechs before him were old models from several seasons back, they were as high as a house and looked very menacing.

Slowly, they circled one another. Both were braced to lash out with what looked like armour-plated fists. Titch studied one mech as it turned away from him. He could see a metal spine within a coil of springs inside the body. The head was slung low on broad shoulders. As the mech continued to move around, still facing its opponent, two red lights glowed from inside the head casing. Titch had to remind himself that he wasn't looking at a living, breathing creature with eyes and limbs, but a machine with a pilot inside.

Through the darkened glass of each mech's chest plate, Titch could just make out a figure at the controls. Wearing a helmet and goggles, each pilot was strapped into a cramped cockpit and surrounded by buttons, screen and switches. Both were grasping joysticks, which they used to carefully control every move the robots made.

Titch looked up and around. A moment later, he spotted the man he had come to see. 'Marshal Johnson,' he said to himself. 'I really hope you're in a good mood.'

Marshal Johnson, the man in charge of the Mech Academy, was watching the two machines from one of the many suspended walkways high up in the hangar. He was wearing a bootlace tie and a cowboy hat. Surrounding him was a group of pilots about the same age as Titch. He looked around, wondering how to get to him.

A steel staircase zigzagged up the far wall. It connected the ground to the walkways. There were guards on the walkway above the entrance, watching the fight. As soon as Titch made a break for the staircase, he knew for sure that he'd be the centre of attention.

'What have I got to lose?' he asked himself, before heading out from his hiding place.

Sprinting across the hangar floor, Titch stayed wide of the two mechs. Both of them continued to rotate slowly, bobbing and weaving at the same time like boxers. He locked his attention on to the staircase and didn't dare look back when the guards began shouting at him.

'Hey!'

'You there!'

'This is a restricted area!'

All of a sudden, the staircase seemed a very long way away. Titch could hear thundering footsteps on the walkways overhead. If he moved quickly, he stood a slim chance of reaching Marshal Johnson before the guards blocked his path. But just then, with a whir of cogs, one of the mechs struck out with its fists. The blow sent the other mech sprawling backwards. Immediately, Titch found himself in its shadow. All he could do was try to throw himself clear as the machine toppled over.

BOOM! The mech hit the ground so hard that the floor underneath it cracked. Titch gasped. It had only just missed him! Picking himself up, he faced the fallen mech. The two red lights were now moving in dizzying spirals. Ignoring the guards' orders to stop right there, Titch bolted once more for the staircase. They had weapons. He knew that. At any moment they could open fire, but this was his one opportunity to reach the Marshal. There was no way he could give up now.

Titch bounded up the steps, but the first guards had already arrived at the top. One of them waited menacingly for him, while another tried to shield Marshal Johnson and the other pilots. Titch may not have looked like a major threat, but every precaution was taken to stop mechs from being stolen or pilots kidnapped for ransom.

'You're in big trouble,' growled the guard who blocked his path.

Titch raised his hands. 'All I want to do is speak to the Marshal. Just give me a minute, please!'

The guard shook his head. 'Trespassers must be punished,' he sneered and took a step towards Titch.

By now several of the guards from the

watchtowers had arrived in the hangar. Hearing footsteps climb the stairs behind him, Titch glanced over his shoulder. He was trapped. He looked around desperately. The fallen mech was just beginning to pick itself up from the floor. It looked a little shaky. Sparks popped from its joints as the pilot moved the machine into an upright position. Looking down from where he was standing, Titch suddenly had an idea. It was a risk, but then what choice did he have?

Grabbing a handrail, he hopped up on to it with both feet, then leapt down on to the back of the mech. The guards watched as the great metal beast wheeled around, but Titch clung on tight. His feet soon found a set of rungs that took him to the mech's waist. The mighty machine attempted to swat him off, but Titch ducked as the huge hand swept by. As the mech stumbled about like someone

bothered by a wasp, Titch seized the chance to make his next move. He waited for the mech to pass near a series of chains that were hanging from the wall of the hangar. Then he reached out for one and jumped on to it. Within seconds, he was sliding to the floor, before racing between the feet of the second mech in a desperate bid to get away.

'OK, kid! I think you've earned my

attention now!' Marshal Johnson called from the walkway at the top of the stairs. 'What's your name?'

Titch took a moment to catch his breath. 'Tommy,' he said. 'But everyone calls me Titch.'

Marshal Johnson looked Titch up and down for a moment. 'So why are you here, Titch?' he said. 'We can't just have people running around in here. These machines are not toys. Get in their way and you run the risk of being squashed like an ant!'

Titch glanced up at the two mechs towering over him and took a deep breath. 'I need a place at the Academy. I want to learn how to be a pilot.'

His words were met by silence. Then, one by one, everyone in the hangar started to laugh.

Marshal Johnson raised his hands in the air to silence them. 'Well, you've missed your shot this time,' he said. 'The trial for places was some time ago . . .'

'But . . . but I've been helping my mother on our ranch,' said Titch. 'She needed me to round up the cattle on my horse and take them to market.'

Again, more laughter filled the hangar.

The Marshal fiddled with his bootlace tie. He was clearly deep in thought.

'So you know how to ride?' he asked finally.

'Sure,' said Titch. 'My horse is kind of wild, but I've learnt how to master her.'

Beside Marshal Johnson, a boy with steely blue eyes and short blond hair started sniggering. Johnson turned and frowned at him.

'This is no laughing matter, Alexei,' he warned the boy. 'Trespassing on Academy grounds is a serious offence.' The boy apologised and looked at his feet.

'I'm sorry,' said Titch. 'I was stupid to think I could join.'

'It was stupid,' agreed Marshal Johnson, tipping back the brim of his hat. 'Very stupid. But you've just shown the kind of bravery that I rarely see in new pilots. Now you've only missed a few days of the new term. There are still weeks to go. Maybe, just maybe, I'll give you a chance.'

Titch crossed his fingers behind his back. 'I won't let you down,' he promised.

Marshal Johnson sighed to himself. Then he nodded at Titch.

'If you pull another crazy stunt like that, you'll be back on your mother's cattle ranch in a flash, but for now, you're in. Congratulations, Titch. You've just gone and earned yourself a place at Mech Academy!'

● ● ●

2

The Underground Bunker

'Really? You mean you'll let me in? Just like that?'

Titch could not believe what he was hearing. A term at the Mech Academy was highly sought after. It was the only way to learn how to pilot a mech and then qualify for the Battle Championship. Only there could you learn how to fight with real mechs — the sort they had in the Championship rounds. Could it really be this simple?

'Well, it's certainly not the usual way to get a place, I'll give you that.' Marshal Johnson raised his hand in the air. 'But I like a boy who's prepared to take risks.'

'But Marshal J, that's not fair,' moaned Alexei, the blond boy who'd laughed earlier.

'Enough,' Marshal Johnson said. 'My decision is final. This boy will be joining you all from here on out, and that's that. What did you say your surname was again?'

'I didn't,' said Titch. 'But it's Darwin – Tommy Darwin. Titch for short.'

Marshal Johnson let out a low whistle. 'I thought you looked familiar . . .'

'People sometimes say I look a bit like my dad, but I wouldn't know about that. I haven't seen him in years.'

The Marshal didn't answer, but he nodded like he understood.

'OK, Titch, well, why don't you go and unpack? Martha and Finn will show you to your sleeping quarters.' He turned to two young apprentices at his side, before glancing at his watch. 'Lessons begin again tomorrow at first light.'

Then he turned on his heels, muttering under his breath. 'Darwin . . . Who'd have thought I'd hear that name again?'

•

'So do you think the Marshal knew your dad?' the boy, Finn, asked finally, as he and Martha led Titch off in the direction of a small, windowless building near the airstrip. Even before Martha and Finn had introduced themselves, it was clear that they were twins. They shared the same pleasant smile, sharp cheekbones and almond-shaped eyes. Titch also noticed how they exchanged the occasional glance, as if reading each other's mind.

'I dunno.' Titch shrugged. 'But a long, long time ago my dad certainly was an apprentice here at Mech Academy. He passed with flying colours and set out with his mech on the Battle Championship trail.'

'Just like we're hoping to do,' said

Martha. 'With luck, we'll qualify to fight in the new season. I can't wait to travel across the country, stopping off at a different battleground each weekend. It'll be like a dream come true.'

'Well, for our family, it's been more like a bad dream,' said Titch. 'Dad may have been the outright winner in the first two seasons, but he never made it through the third. One weekend, midway through the season, he just disappeared.'

Martha raised her eyebrows. 'So what happened?' she asked, looking concerned as they reached the building. Steel doors opened automatically to reveal a spiral staircase.

'It's a mystery,' said Titch, peering down to where the steps opened out into a network of brightly-lit rooms, engineering workshops and corridors. It was a vast underground bunker.

Titch looked back at his feet for a

moment. He barely remembered his father. Even so, he still found it hard to talk about him. He turned back to the twins. 'Dad just never showed up at the next battleground on the Championship calendar,' he said quietly. 'Until I know what happened for sure, I refuse to believe he's gone for good. That's why I'm here. If I can graduate from Mech Academy and join the Championship trail, I might just find out the truth.'

There was silence as the three students walked down the stairs and into a corridor. Once they reached their dorm, Finn showed Titch his bed, which was little more than a hammock, but at least there was a locker for his stuff. And besides, he had no complaints. In fact, he couldn't think of anywhere else that he'd rather be.

'I still can't believe I made it,' he said, unzipping his bag.

'Nor can we!'

'You know, what you did back there was incredible,' said Martha. 'I'm looking forward to seeing what you can do with a mech once you're inside the cockpit and behind the controls!'

'So what's training been like so far?' Titch asked.

'Let's just say there's a lot to learn,' Finn told him.

'Finn is hoping to be a test pilot,' Martha continued. 'He prefers fine-tuning mechs to fighting in them!'

'And my sister's into fixing them up,' added Finn. 'She plans to be a mech engineer. We just need the third member – a pilot – to make us a complete Battle Championship team this season.'

'Well, I just hope I'm OK as a pilot and that I don't disappoint Marshal Johnson once I get behind the controls!' said Titch.

'You certainly can't afford to make mistakes,' warned Martha. 'Only the best students graduate from the Mech Academy.'

'And competition is fierce,' said Finn. He lowered his voice so he couldn't be overheard. 'In fact, some people will do anything to make the grade, and that includes cheating. You can trust us, Titch, but watch out for those who don't play by the rules.'

'Thanks for the advice,' said Titch. 'And good luck to you both!'

•

The three of them slept well that night. When they awoke the next morning, Titch, Finn and Martha went up to join the other students. Marshal Johnson was waiting for them, standing outside the main doors. Behind him, lined up across the runway, stood a row of mechs. These machines had been retired from use in the Battle Championship long ago. Now they were used for training purposes only. To cover up the signs of rust, every mech had been spray-painted in bright colours. Stairs led to each cockpit, which were ready for the pilots. Titch couldn't wait to get started.

'OK, as an introduction to your training,' the Marshal began, 'we have watched veterans from the Battle Championship put these machines through their paces. Today, no matter what kind of team member you plan to be, it's your turn.'

A hum of excited chatter rose up from the group.

'Awesome,' Finn whispered to Titch.

'It's going to be quite a ride,' added Martha.

The Marshal raised his hand, commanding their silence.

'But first we must go over the basics for the benefit of any newcomers,' he continued, without looking at Titch. 'Would anyone care to explain the Battle Championship rules?'

Several hands shot up among the students.

'Easy,' said one, when the Marshal nodded at him. 'Two mechs fight it out until one gets knocked down and doesn't get up again.'

The Marshal didn't look very impressed with this answer. 'OK, well, let me refresh your memories in more detail,' he said. 'Battle rounds take place at the weekend, and in a different location each time. The battleground might be anything from an abandoned nuclear power plant to a bombed-out naval yard. You could even find yourselves fighting in an empty city district or way out in the wilderness. The war was responsible for ruining a lot of places, but we make full use of them all.'

Titch nodded. He was too young to remember his dad talk about the Championship, but he had heard all the stories. School friends who travelled to watch would always return with tales that left him wide-eyed with wonder.

He glanced at the mechs. Each one was fully customisable – he knew that much. You started with the basic body, and then attached weapon-fitted arms and legs that were suited to the terrain. A battleground with cliffs or skyscrapers would need a mech with climbing abilities. Open spaces would be better suited to guns that could shoot long range.

'How many rounds do we fight each Championship weekend?' asked a girl near the front.

'That depends on how good a fighter you are,' the Marshal explained. 'We're talking about knockout rounds, with points awarded to the winner. So you could get knocked out in the first round, or go on to fight three rounds in total and walk away with maximum points.'

'I have a question,' said a boy at the back of the group. 'Do the pilots ever get hurt?'

The Marshal shook his head. He looked amused, as if he'd heard this many times before.

'Only the machines get damaged,' he answered. 'All cockpits are reinforced and armour-plated, you see. But let me tell you something, son, if you're worried about your safety, this probably isn't the sport for you. You might be protected, but you need to control that mech like it's your own body. If you want victory, then you need to take it to the extreme. There's big prize money to be won after all. But lastly, before I ask each of you to climb inside a mech, what is it that a Championship contender seeks more than anything else?'

'Ooh, I know!' Martha shot her hand up in the air, only for her brother to answer for her.

'We fight for honour!'

Marshal Johnson beamed. 'Very good. Now perhaps you two would like to lead the way to the mechs. There aren't any weapons fitted at the moment. Lessons in combat will follow once you've gained complete control of your machines.'

Like all the young apprentices, Titch followed the twins towards the airstrip with a rising sense of excitement. As he walked, the blond boy – Alexei – pushed past him.

'Out of my way, newbie,' he snarled at Titch. 'I've been waiting a long time to fire up one of these!'

'Hey!' cried Martha, who had seen the boy barge through. 'Calm down, Alexei. There are enough mechs for us all.'

'But some are better than others,' he replied with a mocking grin. 'Just as boys make better contenders than girls!'

Without thinking, Titch grabbed Alexei by the shoulder and spun him round.

'That's not true,' he said, squaring up to the boy despite being half his size. 'It's just rude!'

'Leave it, Titch!' Martha pleaded, and tried to pull him away. 'I can handle idiots like Alexei myself, thanks very much.'

Titch continued to glare at Alexei. 'You should apologise to her,' he growled.

At first, Alexei looked shocked. Then he stepped even closer to Titch until he was towering over him. 'Go on then,' he sneered. 'Make me!'

Titch drew breath to respond just as a sharp whistle cut through the air.

'That's enough!' Marshal Johnson called across to them. 'The only fights I

want to see around here are between mechs. Now choose a machine each and climb inside the cockpit!'

Alexei glowered at Titch once more before shoving him to the ground.

'You're going down, little worm!' he snarled. 'I promise you that.'

3

Mastering the Mechs

By the time Titch picked himself up, every other student had rushed to claim a mech. It left him with just one, which looked more beaten up than any of the others. It was dented in places and dotted with welded steel patches. The blue and lime-green panelling did little to cover the rust. Most striking of all was a charred slash that crossed the machine's visor. Some kind of laser weapon had clearly caused the damage and left the mech with a visible battle scar.

'You look like you've seen some great fights in your time,' Titch said as he climbed the steps. 'Let's hope you see some more.'

Inside the cockpit, Titch strapped the harness across his chest and locked it into place. As he did so, the steps automatically retracted. Finally, with a hiss of steam, the dark glass chest plate closed and sealed him in from the outside world.

Titch glanced around at the control panels. It looked completely baffling. Reaching for the headset, he positioned the microphone piece in front of his mouth. Next he put on the helmet and closed the clear plastic visor. Immediately, the scanning laser inside broadcast a steam of data across it. This confirmed that his mech had one hundred per cent power and health. Just then, Titch's earpiece crackled into life.

'OK, listen up,' said Marshal Johnson's voice. 'If everyone is sitting comfortably, then we'll begin. I want you to start by locating the button in front of you marked

"Mech Link". This is the most important button inside your cockpit. It allows you to communicate with the on-board computer. This is basically your co-pilot. It listens. It understands. It speaks. It can answer every question you put to it. Most importantly, it will show you how to pilot your mech. So, before you place your hands upon the controls, press the button and say hi to your new best friend.'

Titch did as he was instructed. 'Hello?' he said as the light beside the button he pressed switched from red to green. 'Can you hear me?'

'Loud and clear,' replied a robotic voice inside his earpiece. 'This is your on-board computer speaking. You can call me LoneStar, but I'm afraid the name of this mech is a mystery to me. All I can say is that this old tin can is a veteran of the Battle Championship. It's just a shame I can't remember any stories of the legendary fights we've won. My memory banks were wiped on retirement and the system rewired for training purposes. Still, in the right hands we can pack a punch!'

Titch smiled to himself.

'Well, LoneStar, I'll do my best.'

'You'll have to do more than that to impress me,' replied the on-board computer. 'Now just follow every word I say and I'll steer you all the way to graduation!'

Marshal Johnson was standing at the doors to the bunker. Over on the runway, the first mechs were lurching into life. They looked a little unsteady on their feet. One jerked forward several steps and then halted, as if the engine inside had stalled. Another went backwards, obviously by accident, while a third began to stagger around in circles.

Marshal Johnson closed his eyes for a

moment, as if he couldn't bear to watch. Just then, as one mech after another continued to lurch into life, the Marshal's attention was drawn to the blue-and -green machine at the far end. It had yet to move.

'There's always one who's no good at all,' he muttered quietly. 'Whoever it is we'll have to send home early.'

Inside his mech, Titch was taking his time. He wanted to feel comfortable with the controls, rather than risk making a mistake. Eventually, he took a deep breath.

'It's now or never,' he said to himself, before pushing the control sticks forward. Immediately, the mech started to move. 'This is crazy!' Titch cried as the cockpit shuddered with every step the giant machine took. 'It's like I'm on a stormy sea!'

'Steady as you go,' replied LoneStar. 'Don't lose concentration!'

As soon as Titch had grasped the control sticks, the projection on the inside of his visor added a new layer – a camera feed from the mech's head. Not only that, but Titch found that by looking around, the camera would swivel in the same direction. It gave Titch a clear view of what was going on outside.

'OK,' he said excitedly, tightening his grip on the sticks. 'Let's see what this thing can really do!'

'Easy does it,' warned the computer as Titch pushed his mech into a run. 'You really need to follow my instructions and . . . whoa!'

But it was too late. Titch was already on his way!

•

For weeks, Marshal Johnson's young apprentices worked hard at learning the basics of mech control. Eventually, the apprentices were divided into two groups.

Those who planned on becoming engineers, like Martha, were taken off for training by Marshal Johnson's technical tutors, leaving the pilots behind, who were sorted into pairs. Finally, it was time to learn how to fight.

When the Marshal put Titch with Alexei, Titch couldn't help wondering if he'd done it deliberately because they hadn't hit it off. Even so, Alexei seemed delighted by the choice. Before heading back to their mechs, he turned to Titch and told him to be ready.

'It's time to learn respect for those who could crush you!' he hissed. 'I've been watching you, Titch. Prepare to be defeated!'

'Bring it on,' Titch replied. 'I won't go down without a fight!'

Titch climbed the steps to his cockpit. He might be much smaller than Alexei, but inside a mech they were equal.

'Is everything OK?' asked LoneStar. 'That boy looks like trouble.'

'I'm sure I'll meet far worse if I ever make it into the Battle Championship,' said Titch, strapping himself into his seat. 'Let's show him what we can do.'

The on-board computer folded the steps and sealed the cockpit doors. At the same time, several switches lit up on the control panel overhead that Titch hadn't seen before.

'You need to set us up for fight mode,' said LoneStar. 'The Marshal's right – you seem to have a rare talent. Let's see what you can do in battle.'

Titch followed the instructions. He pressed one switch and the mech rolled its shoulders before lowering its head. Another switch made it curl its steel claw hands into fists. By the time he had reached the final switch, the mech was battle-ready.

'Wow,' said Titch as he turned the metal beast to face his opponent. 'Round one, here we come!'

• • •

4

Let Battle Commence

The two mechs squared up to each other.

Alexei's mech swung the first punch. It was wild and unguided. Even so, it hit Titch's mech full-on. Titch responded with a counterblow that knocked Alexei's machine backwards a step. As the two mechs started to slug it out, Titch found himself being thrown about like a rodeo rider astride an angry bull. He was in control of every move his machine made, and yet the jolts and lurches were hard on his body.

'I need to toughen up,' he yelled as Alexei's mech caught him with a blow.

'You're doing fine,' replied LoneStar. 'Damage levels are holding. Health and power OK. Just watch out for those punches, Titch. He's a tough fighter and I'd be very sorry if he floored you. I hate to see my apprentice students fail at the first hurdle.'

'No chance,' said Titch as he spun his mech out of harm's way. 'This match is mine!'

With that, he turned and slammed his machine into the other boy's mech. It was a full-on body blow. The impact rattled through the cockpit, but Titch's attention was locked on the camera feed. It seemed the move had been enough to knock his opponent into the dust.

'You did it!' cried LoneStar, so loudly that the cockpit speakers rattled.

Titch steered his mech back a step. He wanted a clear view of the toppled mech. Then another voice crackled into his earpiece. It was Alexei. 'I'm hurt. It's really bad. I was thrown out of my seat in the fall. Now I can't move my legs!'

'What?' Titch was panicked. 'But these cockpits are armour-plated!'

'I don't think I was strapped in correctly,' Alexei croaked. 'Help me, Titch. Please!'

Without hesitation, Titch shut down his mech's fight mode and snapped out of his harness. 'Open the cockpit doors and lock the steps into place!' he commanded LoneStar. 'I'm going out there!'

Titch's heart was pounding as he rushed down the stairs. All around him, mechs were battling it out in pairs. The air was thick with the dust that they had kicked up. Alexei's mech was sprawled on the airstrip in front of him. Titch hit the ground and sprinted towards the hulking metal beast. Suddenly it rose up without warning. All Titch could do was dive to one side as it stepped past him and advanced towards his mech. 'What are you doing?' he cried out and then gasped when Alexei's mech slammed a double-fisted swipe into the side of his machine. With nobody at the controls, Titch's mech simply crumpled in a shower of sparks.

'Victory!'

Stunned, Titch turned to see Alexei

emerge from his cockpit and punch the air. He watched the mech's steps extend towards him and the support struts drop into place. When he looked back up, Alexei was still making the most of the moment.

'You said you were hurt,' Titch called up to him. 'That's cheating!'

'The win belongs to me,' crowed Alexei, holding both hands over his head.

Titch looked back at his mech. It had literally collapsed on the spot, but then the two red lights behind its visor blinked back into life. Despite the fights going on around him, he could just about hear LoneStar's voice running systems checks inside the cockpit. It was a relief to know that at least his mech wasn't too badly damaged. Even so, Titch feared that losing out to Alexei would have him marked down.

He looked around. Marshal Johnson was still observing from the edge of the airstrip. He caught Titch's eye, then wrote something on a clipboard. Titch sighed to himself and kicked at the dusty ground. He wouldn't fall for the same trick again.

When the last mechs had finished fighting, Marshal Johnson instructed every pilot to dismount and gather round him. Titch trudged over with a heavy heart. This was not the start he'd been hoping for.

'Some of you did well,' the Marshal began, with a nod to Alexei. 'Others, not so good,' he added as Titch looked at his feet. 'All of you have a long way to go in your training. Today has just been the start. Now head back to the bunker and get some rest. I guarantee you will be feeling very bruised by this evening.'

As the young apprentices turned to leave, Titch glanced back at Marshal Johnson. The Marshal was studying him closely. He beckoned Titch over as the others headed for the bunker doors.

'Between you and me, I'm surprised Alexei got the better of you back there,' he said. 'You were on course for a win. What happened? Did he take you out on the blind side?'

'Something like that,' said Titch with a shrug. As much as he disliked what the other boy had done, he wasn't a sneak.

He was about to promise that he'd do better next time when a cry from the watchtower drew the Marshal's attention. Several guards had drawn their weapons and were aiming at something approaching from outside the main gates. Titch saw an eight-legged mech crawl into view. The gates were locked, but the mech continued to close in. Several more could be seen crawling along behind it. When one of the guards threatened to open fire, the Marshal ordered them to stand down and open up.

'A spider mech means trouble, and I

know who's behind it,' he said. 'The last thing I want is a gunfight on these grounds, so it's best we play nice for now. Let them in so I can speak to the man in charge.'

• • •

5

Unwelcome Guests

The leading spider mech was much larger than the machines behind it. Even so, they all looked a menacing sight to Titch. He stood firm beside Marshal Johnson, who didn't move as the visitors crawled to a halt in front of them. Together they watched as the hatch on the leading mech spun open. Then a head popped up into the sunshine.

'Such a fine place you have here, Marshal,' said the man who appeared. He was wearing a skunk-skin hat, the pelt striped white from brow to tail, and a buck-hide jacket trimmed with tassels. 'Me and the boys thought we'd drop in to

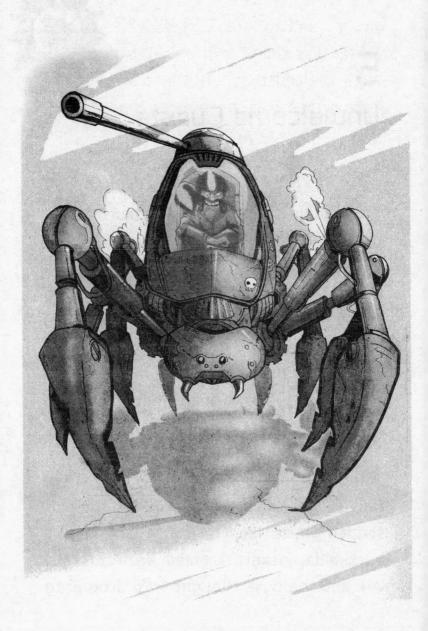

say hi. Isn't that right, fellas?' He turned to address the line of mechs behind him. Titch noticed that all the machines were pockmarked where bullets had struck them. They looked like they'd seen some tough times. So too did the ragtag bunch of cowboys who began to climb out.

'Wyatt Thorne,' growled the Marshal. 'Aren't you supposed to be behind bars?'

The man spread his hands wide and looked offended. 'Now is that any way to greet a former Championship contender?' he asked, before hopping out of his mech. 'How many seasons did we fight before you retired to set up this Academy? Was it four? Five? You and I go back a long way.'

'We do indeed,' growled the Marshal. 'Way back to the day you were expelled from the Battle Championship for sabotaging my mech!'

Wyatt Thorne's great brow knitted together. He smoothed his drooping moustache with one hand. Then he grinned, revealing a front tooth made from gold. 'So you still think I was out to wreck your Championship bid, do you?'

'I sure do. You were caught cutting the wires to the safety sensors on my mech. What could be more proof than that? It could've caused a fatal accident. If you hadn't been caught red-handed, I might've died in battle!'

'Well, I served my time,' said Wyatt Thorne, looking uneasy before glancing over his shoulder at the gang behind him. 'OK, so I didn't serve all of it. These guys needed me on the outside to lead a little gun-smuggling operation. They organised a jailbreak, and here I am. An outlaw with my very own posse now – my Wired Bunch.'

'So what do you want, Wyatt?' Marshal Johnson growled.

Titch thought that it sounded like the

Marshal's patience was running out.

'Just a little look around,' said Wyatt. 'Your students are training in some nice old mechs, aren't they?' he added as his gaze settled on the machines. 'They'd fetch quite a good old price broken down for spare parts, right? Apart from that one,' he added, pointing at Titch's mech. 'That hunk of junk has seen better days. I don't suppose you could even give it away!'

'Hey!' cried Titch.

'You need to leave,' replied Marshal Johnson. 'Every single guard in this Academy has a weapon pointing at you. All I have to do is give the word.'

Wyatt Thorne grinned. He held the Marshal's gaze for a moment, before switching his attention to Titch. His eyes narrowed. 'Have we met before, kid?'

'No, no, we haven't,' said Titch.

'He's just an apprentice,' said the Marshal. 'Leave him alone. Climb back inside your spider mechs and beat it.'

In response, Wyatt Thorne stepped closer to Titch. His Wired Bunch quickly jumped off their mechs and joined him. All of a sudden, Titch felt quite threatened.

'You look so familiar,' growled Thorne. 'And not in a good way. Now are you going to tell me your name, or do I have to beat it out of you . . . OW!'

Marshal Johnson had heard enough. In one sure move, perfected from years of teaching mech attack techniques, he had grabbed Wyatt Thorne, swept his legs from under him and left him with his face in the dirt and a boot on his back.

'Get off me!' complained the outlaw.

'Not until you promise to get out of here,' demanded Marshal Johnson. 'And take these goons as well. You blew your chance to compete in the Battle Championship. Now let the next generation make their mark!'

And with that, he lifted his boot. Thorne dusted himself down. Then, with a final glare at the Marshal and Titch, he turned on his heel and left. His sidekicks followed on behind him. As Wyatt passed a noticeboard, he paused to swipe a sheet of paper from it. Marshal Johnson scowled, his patience tested. It wasn't until the line of spider mechs were a speck in the distance that he turned back to Titch.

'What was all that all about?' asked Titch.

Marshal Johnson sighed. 'I wasn't going to tell you just yet,' he said. 'But with everything that's just happened, now seems as good a time as any. Wyatt Thorne knew your father, you see. We both did. We fought in several Battle Championship seasons together.'

Titch nodded. It was all beginning to make sense.

'It was your dad who caught Thorne trying to sabotage my mech,' Marshal Johnson explained. 'If he knew your identity, Wyatt would be sure to want revenge.'

'So was Wyatt in jail when my dad went missing?' asked Titch, looking thoughtful.

The Marshal nodded. 'Wyatt couldn't have had a hand in that. Your father just never showed up for the next round.

Everyone knew he was a winner in the making, but he simply vanished into thin air.'

Titch was shocked by so many revelations. Even so, it made him all the more determined to get on the Championship trail himself. It was the only way he could find out what had happened to his dad . . . Once and for all.

● ● ●

6

The Assault Course

Titch was keen to return to his training as soon as he could. For several nights, his encounter with Wyatt Thorne and his Wired Bunch gave him bad dreams. Even though the bunker under the Academy was designed to protect everyone from attack, Titch was sure he hadn't seen the last of them. It was only when he climbed into the cockpit of his mech that he felt truly safe again.

'Good to see you, Titch!' said LoneStar one bright morning. 'So what does the Marshal have in store for us today? I'm ready for anything. This mech can still kick metal butt!'

'Agility training,' said Titch as he

strapped himself in.

'On the assault course?' A crackle of static came out of the speaker, which sounded rather like LoneStar tutting. 'The last student who took me over that left me with a fractured toe stabiliser.'

Titch grinned, and popped on his helmet.

'I can handle it,' he promised. 'So long as you take care of me.'

•

The course was located on the far side of the old air-force base. There, the mechs would have to scramble over a scrap heap, scale a three-storey building, drop down, and then cross to an abandoned warehouse. Inside, the Marshal's support team had carefully lit fires inside steel drums. The mechs were expected to get in through the roof, dropping down through skylights, before finding a way out through thick black smoke. The course looked difficult and dangerous. Even so, Titch was fired up with excitement and couldn't wait for his turn.

'You have half an hour to set the fastest time,' the Marshal informed his young pilots through their headsets. 'Make as many attempts as you wish, but be careful. One wrong move could damage your mech so badly you'll be forced to watch from the sidelines.'

'I hope you're listening, Titch,' muttered LoneStar, before instructing Titch to activate the balance monitoring system. 'You're in control,' he reminded him, 'but if it looks like you're about to make a mistake, the alarm will sound.'

'Understood,' said Titch as the first mech sprinted for the scrap heap. It still surprised Titch how quickly these metal giants could move. With every bound, the machine's joints clanked and pistons hissed while its huge arms pumped the air.

Alexei was the first to go. He launched his mech on to the scrap heap of burnt-out cars and aircraft. Within seconds, using the claw-like hands fitted to every mech for the session, he had scaled the building beyond and was on to the warehouse roof. If Titch stood a chance of beating him, he would have to push his mech to the limit.

When it was his turn to face the assault course, Titch gripped the control sticks tightly.

'Are you ready?' he asked the on-board computer.

'All systems go, Titch. Break a leg . . . Actually, try not to do that!'

Titch thrust the sticks forward. With a huge jolt, the mech rushed towards the scrap heap. Every footstep rattled the bones in Titch's body. He could hear LoneStar complaining, but he couldn't break his concentration to reply. This was about speed and agility.

Having conquered the scrap heap, the building loomed before them. Titch leapt for the fire escape bolted to the wall. The mech grasped at the rungs, which pulled the ladder from its fixings. Titch would have to move quickly to scale it before the whole thing peeled away from the wall. At the top, the camera feed inside his visor showed a column of thick smoke rising from the warehouse. There were two ways to reach it. The previous mech had clambered down the other side of the building and then climbed up the wall of the warehouse. Thinking fast, Titch decided there had to be a quicker way.

'We're going to jump,' he said, and pushed his mech into a sprint across the flat rooftop.

'Is this wise, Titch?' asked LoneStar, just as the alarm sounded in the cockpit. 'Clearly not!'

Ignoring the warning, Titch pushed his mech from the edge of the roof. The camera feed showed them rising – and then dropping rather sooner than he'd hoped.

'Uh-oh,' muttered Titch. 'Brace yourself!'

With a metallic-sounding splat, the mech hit the warehouse wall. As it dropped down to the ground, LoneStar groaned as if winded.

'Your engineer has a lot of work ahead of him if you stand a chance of making another attempt,' the on-board computer told Titch. 'Would you like me to radio him?'

'It's a she,' Titch told him, 'and from what I hear from the other students, she's one of the best.'

•

When Martha arrived, Titch was already waiting at the foot of his mech. His machine had been towed off the assault course. It was slumped against the air traffic control tower.

'It isn't as bad as it looks,' he told her. 'LoneStar says two inline cylinders were broken in the fall.'

'I'll deal with it right away.' Martha headed straight for the steps to the cockpit.

Behind them, another mech clambered over the assault course. Smoke continued to pour from the warehouse at the far end. Titch had yet to set a time. He glanced at his watch. Martha wouldn't just have to work quickly, she'd need to perform a miracle!

•

Titch was overjoyed when the red lights behind his mech's visor started glowing once again. He could hear LoneStar communicating with Martha. It sounded like the repairs had been a success. With little time left to put in a time on the assault course, he bounded up the steps to his cockpit.

'Go for it!' said Martha, grabbing her tool kit. 'You can't afford to put a foot wrong!'

Just one mech had attempted another run after Alexei. Titch had watched Finn climb into his cockpit and carefully adjust a panel of dials. It was this kind of attention to detail that would make him such a great test pilot, Titch thought to himself. Once Finn's machine had scaled the wall on to the rooftop and then climbed back down the other side, Titch prepared to follow. He breathed deeply and checked that LoneStar was ready.

'The system is running beautifully,' it told him. 'You were right about your engineer. She's one of a kind!'

Once again, Titch steered his mech towards the scrap heap. The machine crunched over the tangle of metal and quickly scaled the wall of the building.

'Are you feeling lucky?' he asked his on-board computer. 'I'll never set the fastest time by climbing off this rooftop. 'We'll have to try the jump again!'

'Titch! Slow down! You should've learnt from your mistake . . .'

But it was too late. With a lurch, Titch made the mech leap from the edge of the building. For a second or so, it sailed through the air without a single shudder or clank. Titch stretched out the machine's great arms as the warehouse seemed to zoom towards them . . .

With a thunderous crash, the mech hit the wall hard. This time, however, it did so under Titch's control. With the claws of one metal hand grasping the roof, Titch eased the machine upwards. Safely on top, Titch turned his head to locate the skylight. Smoke was billowing up from the inside. Without further thought, Titch dropped his mech into the warehouse. It landed squarely on the floor. Using the camera mountings, he looked around. Something wasn't right. Titch had expected to find burning oil drums. Instead, there was a full-on raging fire!

To his horror, Titch saw that the drums had been tipped over. It meant just one thing. Somebody had started the blaze on purpose.

'We have to get out of here!' Titch cried quickly.

'Temperature sensors are starting to rise inside the cockpit' said LoneStar. 'Be quick before we cook!'

Titch spotted the opening to the warehouse immediately. It was some distance away, but first he had to steer

his mech round a burning stack of crates. As he did so, the foot of his machine connected with an object on the ground. He looked down and gasped.

'Finn!' he cried, instantly recognising his friend's mech. It was sprawled across the warehouse floor, blackened and scorched in places by the fire. 'We have to help!'

Outside, the blaze had come to the attention of Marshal Johnson. Along with the other apprentices, he had rushed to the warehouse. But by then the fire was out of control. It was too hot to even get close. Alexei stood alongside Martha, looking worried as they strained to peer through the smoke.

'I didn't mean it to be this bad,' he muttered under his breath.

'What?' said Martha.

'Er, nothing,' said Alexei, looking sheepish.

But there wasn't time for Martha to ask more as, just then, the sound of a siren told them the Academy's fire truck was racing to the scene.

'There must be something we can do,' said Martha, who was beginning to panic. 'My brother's in there. So is Titch!'

'I'm going in!' cried Alexei, rushing for the entrance before the Marshal could stop him.

The blond-haired boy disappeared into the smoke for a moment, only to back out as the outline of Titch's mech stepped into view. It was carrying another mech in its arms, which it laid out in front of the fire truck. As it stood back, the fallen machine's chest plate cracked open. Smoke billowed out from inside. Some of the students clambered on to the mech to help the pilot out. Finn emerged, looking dazed and coughing.

'We thought it was all over for you!' cried Martha, who rushed to hug her twin brother.

'My mech's cooling system failed!' croaked Finn. 'I'd have been toast if it wasn't for Titch!'

Titch was just climbing out of his cockpit. He stood on the platform, looking down at everyone. Behind the Marshal and his apprentices, a fire truck was in position and firing a water cannon into the warehouse.

'I never got to set a time.' Titch turned to Marshal Johnson and looked back along the assault course.

'It's too late now,' replied the Marshal. 'Besides, I think you've achieved enough for one day.'

'So who was fastest?' asked Martha.

The Marshal checked his clipboard. 'It seems Alexei is our winner,' he said.

'Yes!' cried Alexei, who had been hugely relieved to see that Finn was OK.

The Marshal frowned at him. 'It seems strange that the blaze started so soon after you made your final run,' he said slowly. 'You didn't see anything?'

'Are you accusing me of starting it?' Alexei tried to look offended. 'I'd never dream of such a thing.'

'Hmm.' The Marshal continued to stare at Alexei, but he didn't say anything.

'Let's just say that Finn isn't the only one to make a lucky escape. I won't stand for rule breaking, especially not when it puts people's lives in danger. In the Battle Championship, that kind of stunt can lead to jail.'

Immediately, Titch thought of Wyatt Thorne. He was still troubled by the outlaw, but now it looked like he'd have to be wary of Alexei, too. He couldn't be sure that the boy was behind the blaze, but there was definitely something shifty about him. If Titch was going to make it to the Championship, he'd have to watch his back . . .

● ● ●

7

Weapon Practice

For the next couple of weeks, the young apprentices spent more time inside their trainer mechs than on the ground. Like everyone else, Titch worked hard at mastering the controls, and fighting hand-to-hand, until finally the Marshal decided that everyone was ready for their mechs to be fitted with weapons. The students gathered in the same hangar where Titch had first sneaked in. No mechs were present. Instead, a very long steel-topped table had been wheeled into position. What was laid out from one end to the other took the students' breath away.

'Awesome,' said Alexei, staring at the

huge range of missiles, grab hooks and guns of every size and shape.

The students started chattering excitedly. The Marshal raised his hand and waited for silence.

'In the wrong hands, these can be deadly,' he reminded them sternly. 'Now I want everyone to regroup on the walkway before this lesson can begin. Safety first at all times, people.'

Titch climbed the stairs with Finn.

'So, have you ever watched a Battle Championship round?' Titch asked.

'Once,' Finn said. 'They came to a city near us. My older brother took me.'

'What was it like?'

Finn looked lost in thought for a moment. Then a big grin crossed his face. 'It was amazing. Two mechs were fighting each other on the roof of an old shopping mall. It went on for hours. Everything from the noise to the explosions was intense!

I've never seen anything like it before. From that moment on, I knew the Battle Championship was for me!'

Titch nodded. Since joining the Academy, he had really found a passion for piloting these huge machines. Even so, he couldn't lose sight of the fact that he was really doing all this in the hope that he might track down his father. In a way, working hard to perfect his skills left him feeling closer to his dad than ever before . . .

As the apprentices gathered on the walkway, Marshal Johnson faced the hangar entrance and waved his arm.

'OK. Bring it on!'

By now the sound of slow but thundering footsteps was familiar to the students. When a great shadow fell across the floor of the hangar, they knew what was coming next. The mech strode in, towering over the table. A small group of engineers followed the giant machine inside. They fanned around it and carefully removed two pulse guns from the table. Using ladders to stand on, they didn't take long to fix them to the mech's wrists. Special connectors allowed them to snap the weapons into place. When the mech was ready, it took a step back and spun its wrists around and around for a few seconds.

'Wow,' said Titch under his breath. He watched in wonder as the mech turned and took aim at something outside the hangar.

'Cover your ears,' the Marshal warned. 'This could be loud!'

A moment later, two bright globes of light began to build in the barrel of each gun. Electricity flickered inside each globe. The mech then pulled both triggers. With a deafening spit, both balls of energy shot out of the hangar. The explosion, some distance away, returned a cloud of light and heat that caused the students to shield their eyes.

'OK,' said Finn. 'That was loud!'

The Marshal turned to face them.

'These mechs are armour-plated. Such a strike might knock out their system-control unit, but the pilots will always be safe inside,' he told them. 'Just remember that in a Battle Championship round, if your mech takes on so much damage that it can't rise again, you've lost.'

•

Over the next few training sessions, the apprentice engineers learnt how to select a weapon and bolt it on to the mech. The pilots spent time inside the cockpit practising target aim and lock-on techniques in a vast crater to one side of the airbase. It was as big as a quarry, thanks to the bomb that had exploded there during the war. As a result, the steep rock walls provided a safe place for the mechs to try out their firepower. And what firepower they possessed!

'We're weapon-ready,' Titch told LoneStar that morning. 'Let's see what we can do!'

Without waiting for the on-board computer to reply, Titch spun his machine around. Straight away, he found a target spray-painted on to a rock across the crater. Titch lined it up in his sights. Then he took a breath and pulled the trigger.

'Wooohoooo!'

Martha had fitted his mech with two NailStormers. Titch knew these were basically machine guns that fired steel darts with explosive tips. He'd just never seen them in use until now. He watched a flock of darts sail through the air. They did so silently, only to burst into a ball of flames on hitting the target.

'Good shot!' said LoneStar. 'Just watch

out for your fellow students. Some of them look very trigger-happy!'

Sure enough, all around the crater, the apprentice pilots were using their mechs to fire weapons at targets. Some were trying out long-range snipers; others fired grapple hooks high into the wall of the crater which they used to practise climbing up and down. Titch watched Alexei with interest. He had selected a single CannonBlaster 2.0. You could only fire the weapon twice before returning to your engineer to reload. Even so, it packed a punch. The CannonBlaster 2.0 was a heavy piece of equipment. It was a risky thing to choose as it slowed a mech down, but just one direct hit could take out an opponent.

Finding himself with enough space, Alexei warned his fellow students through their headsets that he was about to fire. Everyone paused their mechs and watched. Unlike Titch's NailStormers, which were

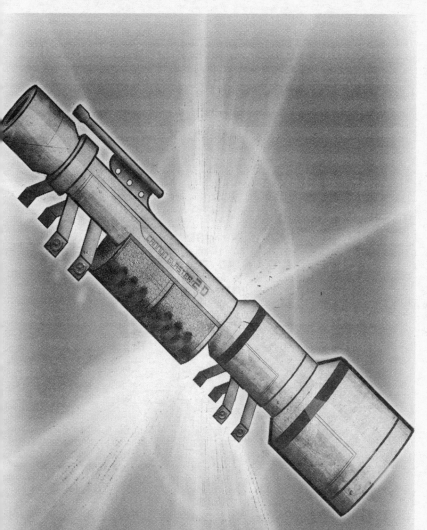

CannonBlaster 2.0

long and sleek, Alexei's chosen weapon was so big it looked like it had been wrenched from the turret of a tank. Such was its power that when he pulled the trigger, the kickback knocked his mech off its feet. Nobody had a chance to laugh, however, because the explosion on the far side of the crater was intense. With an earth-shaking boom, a cloud shaped like a mushroom rose into the air. Then chunks

of rock came raining down across the crater.

'Ouch!' complained LoneStar as a small boulder bounced off the mech's head. 'Thank goodness for a titanium skull!'

In his earpiece, Titch could hear his fellow pilots chuckling at what had just happened to Alexei. His mech was sprawled flat on its back in the dirt. It struggled to get up, waving its metal limbs uselessly.

But Titch remained grim-faced. For something else had caught his attention in his mech's camera feed – something gleaming in the sunshine, way beyond the airbase, up in the mountain crags.

'What is that?' he muttered to himself.

LoneStar didn't respond. The on-board computer was too busy checking the mech's system hadn't sustained any damage from the rock shower. Even so, Titch struggled to shake off the strange feeling that they were being watched . . .

● ● ●

8
Wyatt's Revenge

Wyatt Thorne stood on top of his eight-legged spider mech. He had positioned his machine on the mountain scarp that overlooked the Mech Academy. In his hands, he was clutching a device that looked like an old brass-plated telescope. He held it up to his eye. As he did so, a tiny laser beam shot from the lens on the other end. It was powerful, as you'd expect from an Angledrop optical laser sight, and stretched out high over the walls of the airbase. Next, he pulled a lever on the side of the telescope. Immediately, the far end of the beam switched down towards the ground. Through the viewfinder, it

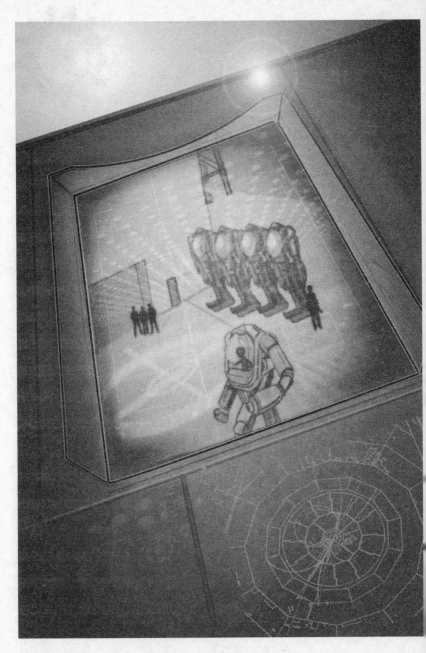

delivered a perfect overhead shot of the training grounds. The outlaw turned a wheel beside the lever and the optical beam began to sweep between hangars.

'Come out, come out, wherever you are . . .'

When Wyatt found what he was looking for, he grinned so broadly it pushed creases into his stubbly cheeks.

'Well, how about that!' he growled to himself. 'Those nice mechs are loaded up with weapons too. Not a bad day's work if we can get our hands on them. They should fetch a good price over the border.'

The outlaw adjusted the lever once more. This time, the Angledrop view glided across to the side of the crater. There stood Marshal Johnson.

'It's payback time,' growled Wyatt. 'Nobody humiliates me without paying a price!'

Shutting down the telescope beam, he

turned and faced the other way. A band of smaller spider mechs were gathered on the rocks behind him. Most displayed the scars of welding work. All were fitted with weapons, including Electromagnetic Lassos. These jet-propelled, coiled metal loops could jam any robotic system control when pulled tight around them. On seeing that their leader was preparing to address them, the spider mechs rose to attention.

'You've been loyal to me, my Wired Bunch,' Wyatt said. 'Now it's time I showed my thanks.' He tipped his tracker's hat back with one finger. Then he jabbed his thumb over his shoulder. 'There are more mechs down there than I imagined. We'll get a high price for them all. Every one of you could be rich by nightfall!'

Pacing across the roof of the mech, Wyatt gestured at the old airbase behind him. 'The Academy is heavily guarded, so this is the plan,' he told them, before pausing to whip out a folded sheet of paper from his pocket. 'On my last visit I managed to take a copy of the Academy's training timetable. I know for a fact that the students are expected to train in the mech simulator later today. Once they head down to the bunker, that's when we strike. I want half of you to stay here and throw as much firepower into that airbase as you can. Cause havoc and confusion, my friends! The rest of you come with me. We'll ride in, lasso their mechs and drag them away. Now who's with me?'

A show of hands told him all that he needed to know.

Wyatt Thorne peered at the old airbase behind him. It shimmered in the heat haze. Vultures circled overhead.

'Then, as soon as the students head for the bunker,' he muttered, 'we strike.'

● ● ●

9
Ambush!

Weapons training had proved to be a big hit among the young apprentices. At the same time, Titch, along with everyone else, was feeling tense about what would follow as the term drew to a close. The next session would take place in the bunker, inside a mech cockpit simulator. It sounded like fun, but everyone knew this was where the Marshal would decide whether or not they were fit to join the Battle Championship. The simulator allowed them to fight in computerised versions of all the battlegrounds on the trail. It would also put them up against some of the legends of the sport. As a test, it was one of the toughest they would face.

'The time has come,' said Marshal Johnson as they left their mechs behind and headed for the bunker. 'If anyone hopes to earn their wings, I expect them to gain top marks.'

As the last of his apprentices took to the spiral staircase, he looked around to see that two had yet to follow.

'Titch and Alexei,' he called across to the boys. 'The simulator session starts in fifteen minutes. You really should come inside to prepare.'

Titch was standing on the platform of his mech. His cockpit was open. He had climbed out to leave, only for his attention to be drawn by the target he'd been firing at. The rock was blackened where he'd hit it. What he'd missed by a centimetre or two was the bullseye, and that left him unsatisfied.

'Give me another five minutes,' he pleaded with the Marshal. 'I can't leave until I've nailed the target.'

Marshal Johnson looked set to order him inside. Then he smiled to himself. 'How about you, Alexei?' he asked.

The boy had followed the others out of the crater. Unlike them, however, he had hung back to watch Titch from the top step.

'I'd like to stay and watch,' he said. 'Titch is a natural. I realise that now. Maybe I'll pick up some tips.' He looked uncomfortable as he said the words, like he didn't really mean it, but Marshal Johnson didn't seem to notice.

'Very well,' said the Marshal. 'Just don't be late. This simulator session is vital if you want a future as a Battle Championship contender.'

He turned and headed for the spiral staircase. As he stepped inside the building that housed it, the steel doors closed automatically behind him.

Alexei returned his attention to the quarry. Titch had already climbed back inside his mech. The blond-haired boy watched as he moved his mech further back from the target. Clearly, he was making it even harder for himself. Alexei was impressed. Knowing Titch was about to shoot at the target, he covered his ears with his hands.

A moment later, before Titch could fire, something dropped out of the sky with a whoosh and landed at the feet of his mech. Alexei peered across the crater at the object. It looked like a metal apple – and that only meant one thing. His eyes widened in horror.

'Quick, Titch!' he yelled. You have to get out of there. That thing is going to explode!'

•

Inside the cockpit, the mech's threat detection sensors identified the device as a Lob Bomb. LoneStar knew just what that meant.

'Uh-oh,' it said as one of the screens inside the cockpit flashed a warning.

Titch glanced at the screen, which promptly switched to static when the bomb went off.

As the blast wave rocked through the cockpit, the mech staggered backwards and fell to the ground. A second passed before Titch opened his eyes. He looked around. The cockpit lights flickered. Sparks spat from one of the control panels.

'LoneStar?' cried Titch. 'Speak to me!'

'I'm still here,' said the on-board computer after a moment, though it sounded very shocked. 'Rebooting the system . . . now!'

As the lights came back online and the sparks stopped, Titch was relieved to hear the sound of his mech powering up once more. Hurriedly, he scrambled the machine back on to its feet and looked around.

Some distance away, on the far side of the crater, another Lob Bomb detonated. Once again, Titch felt the force inside the cockpit and wrestled to keep the mech upright.

'What's going on?' he cried.

'For such a small device,' said LoneStar, 'a Lob Bomb produces a ring of high pressure that simply flattens everything within a twenty-metre circle. No mech can take any more than three hits. We have to get out of this crater! We're being attacked!'

'Then find out who's attacking us!' Titch cried.

He spun the mech and raced for the steps. At the same time, he looked up and around. Yet more Lob Bombs could be seen soaring towards the old airbase. Then a flash caught his eye from high up in the mountains. They were coming from near the summit.

'Spider mechs!' he cried. 'Up there! Look!'

Straight away, LoneStar zoomed in on the mountain scarp. 'Wyatt Thorne is behind this,' said the on-board computer. 'That's his Wired Bunch.'

'Wyatt Thorne?' Titch just knew the outlaw had been up to no good. 'So where is he?' he asked as they reached the top of the steps out of the crater. 'And what's Alexei doing out in the open?' he cried as the other boy filled his camera view. 'He'll get himself killed!'

Immediately, Titch opened up the loudspeaker.

'You can't stay there, Alexei!' he yelled, just as the Marshal reappeared at the bunker's steel doors once more.

'Get in here!' the Marshal shouted.

'Take shelter as fast as you can!'

Alexei looked frozen with fear, cowering as yet another Lob Bomb detonated in the crater. 'Alexei, don't go inside,' started Titch. 'Help me! Get back inside your cockpit!' he tried again. 'We've got an outlaw bombing us. We can't let him destroy everything! Help me hunt him down!'

'Exit your mech and take shelter in the bunker!' Marshal Johnson called from the sidelines. 'Even an ambush can't stop training once we're all safely below ground. Let the guards do their best to fight them off!'

As he said this, the turret of a large spider mech could be seen crawling past the other side of the perimeter wall. It was making its way to the main gates.

'The guards are no match for a machine that menacing!' Titch cried at Alexei. 'Are you with me?'

This time, Alexei seemed to hear him. He looked directly into the camera fixed to the head of Titch's mech. Then he nodded and sprang to his feet . . .

● ● ●

10
Enemy at the Gates

Wyatt Thorne chuckled to himself when the first bullets bounced off his spider mech. Those idiot guards could fire all they liked, but nothing would get through his armour-plated baby. As he crawled towards the main gates, another bullet pinged away uselessly. Wyatt began to feel annoyed. He pulled a lever inside his cockpit. In response, a circular hatch opened up at the front of his mech and a telescopic cannon extended into place. He took aim at one of the watchtowers. The guards scrambled from the tower, with just seconds to spare, before the outlaw destroyed it by firing a Cactus Missile.

Not only that, but the device released a spray of spikes that forced the guards to flee for their lives.

'The Marshal's mechs will be easy pickings!' Wyatt said into his mouthpiece. 'Take as many as you can, boys!'

Behind him trailed the dozen or so smaller spider mechs. The pilots inside confirmed that they understood, which left Wyatt to train his cannon on the main gates. As it turned out, there was no need to fire another Cactus Missile. Just as he was about to hit the launch button, the entrance opened outwards to reveal not one but two of the giant mechs they had hoped to seize.

'Well, what do you know?' muttered Wyatt, preparing to fire the missile anyway. Losing these two mechs wouldn't be such a big deal. Not with so many more inside the airbase. 'Get ready to eat dust, my friends!'

•

Inside the cockpit, Titch heard the alarm sound. It signalled that a threat had locked on to his mech. Quickly, he stabbed at the intercom button. It allowed him to communicate with Alexei.

'Head around to the trees at the foot of the mountains,' Titch instructed him. 'Fire back at them so they stop targeting the airbase and turn their attention on to you!'

'What?' Alexei sounded horrified. 'But I might get hit! Can't you come with me?'

'There's no time. Please, just do it!'

'What are you going to do?' asked Alexei.

'Save our skins, I hope!' shouted Titch.

With that, he thrust his mech towards the spider-like machine. He could see the turret taking aim. He had just a second spare to reach it before his mech took a missile in the face.

'What is it with you and danger?' asked

LoneStar, but there was no time for Titch to reply. Instead, he used his mech to grasp the spider mech's turret, directing as much power into its fists as he could. Then, to the sound of creaking metal, he began to buckle and bend the weapon. A moment later, the turret had a kink in

the middle so it pointed upwards. It was now completely useless. Behind the machine, the Wired Bunch backed away nervously.

'You've seen what my mech can do,' warned Titch. 'Don't make me show you again.'

Titch's earpiece crackled.

'What have you done to my spider mech?' It was Wyatt, who had clearly just hacked into the mech's communication system. 'You'll pay for that!'

'Not this time,' cried Titch, turning his attention to the hatch on top of the spider mech. 'How does this thing open?'

'Twist it,' said LoneStar. 'Like a jam jar!'

Titch locked his mech's great fingers on to the hatch, and turned it anti-clockwise. Sure enough, in a hiss of steam, it popped off the top of the spider mech. Inside, a very nervous-looking outlaw peered up into the mech's camera.

'Can we talk about this?' asked Wyatt. 'There's been a misunderstanding . . .'

As he spoke, Lob Bombs continued to rain down on the Academy. Titch switched his communications link so he could talk directly to Alexei.

'What's going on? Are you OK? Talk to me!'

When Alexei failed to respond, Titch began to worry. It was LoneStar who put his mind at ease, but not in a good way.

'According to his mech's location detector, he's back in the airbase, directly outside the entrance to the bunker. Titch, it looks like he's left you to fight this battle on your own.'

Titch sighed to himself. He'd been a fool to think he could rely on Alexei. Now he'd just have to handle the Wired Bunch on his own. Wyatt, meanwhile, had seized the opportunity to haul an

Electromagnetic Lasso from his cockpit. When Titch looked back, the outlaw had already activated the jet attached to one end of the metal cord. All Wyatt had to do was throw that end high up into the air. As soon as the jet fired, it curled the cord into a loop which opened wide as it shot towards its target.

Titch grasped the controls in a bid to move away, but it was too late. A moment later, the lasso was locked round the mech's waist. Immediately, it created an electromagnetic force field around the machine.

'Gotcha!' crowed Wyatt, quickly throwing the other end of the lasso to the spider mech behind him. 'Go take this one back to the mountains. I'll deal with the boy once I've looted the rest of the mechs!'

Titch tried to pull away, only to find the power inside his machine was struggling just to keep the cockpit lit.

'Can you do anything?' he asked LoneStar.

'You're on your own, soldier!' replied the on-board computer. 'Energy cells have dropped to emergency levels!'

'Just hang in there,' replied Titch, who was already thinking up a plan. 'I'm not giving up that easily.'

Titch popped his seat belt clear and climbed out of his seat. He had to open the cockpit door manually in order to step out on to the platform. This high up, a stiff wind was blowing. Wyatt's mech was smaller than his, but not by much. Even so, it was too far to jump. As the outlaw helped two of his men fix the Electromagnetic Lasso in place below, Titch seized the only chance he had. He reached down for the metal cable where it had pulled tight around his mech, and swung on to it. Using the sleeves of his shirt to protect his hands, he then slid down towards Wyatt as fast as possible.

Wyatt Thorne had no idea that Titch was rocketing towards him. The first he knew of it was when Titch's boots connected with his backside. The impact knocked Wyatt clean off the mech and into the grass.

'I don't give up that easily,' Titch called down to him, unhooking the lasso before Wyatt's men could react.

At once, the mech behind him returned to full power. The automatic steps dropped into place within seconds. Straight away, Titch bounded back up to the cockpit and closed himself inside. Throwing himself into his seat, he grabbed the controls with one task in mind.

A moment later, the outlaw Wyatt Thorne and his Wired Bunch found themselves staring down the barrels of two NailStormers. Without a word, all of them raised their hands in submission.

'Tell your friends up there in the mountains to call a halt to the bombing,' said Titch, addressing them through the mech's loudspeakers. 'This game is over.'

Wyatt glared up at the giant machine before him. Then, with a sigh, he lowered his hands.

'I won't forget this,' said the outlaw, and reached down for his radio.

A moment later, peace returned to the airbase. Abandoning his spider mech with the buckled cannon, Wyatt clambered back on to the machine behind it and slapped the bodywork hard. 'Let's get going,' he growled. Then he turned to Titch. 'If you make it on to the Battle Championship trail, you can be sure you'll be seeing a whole lot more of me!'

'And I'll be ready for you,' said Titch, sounding braver than he felt.

Wyatt Thorne turned on his heels and growled. 'Nobody gets the better of me,' he snarled. 'Even if I have to take my time, you'll pay for what you've done today!'

● ● ●

11

Pass or Fail?

As Titch returned to the Mech Academy, he was worried. He had saved many good machines from the hands of the bandits, but at what price? By the time he got into the bunker, the simulation session was finished. And what was more, Marshal Johnson was nowhere to be seen.

'He's watching film footage from the session,' Martha told Titch. 'Apparently, he likes to see how his students fight from every angle.'

'Nobody's allowed to disturb him until he's finished,' Finn added.

'But I need to explain myself,' said Titch. 'I couldn't just let Wyatt Thorne walk away with our mechs.'

'The Marshal believed his security guards could deal with any threat,' said Martha. 'That's what he told us before we started the session. I don't suppose he'll be happy with the fact that you stayed out there.'

Titch thought back to how helpless the guards had been when Wyatt aimed his gun turret at the watchtower. The Marshal must've underestimated how much firepower Wyatt Thorne was packing. Had he known the outlaw's mech was armed with Cactus Missiles, surely he would've ordered everyone to defend the Academy?

One thing was for sure, though. It didn't sound as if the Marshal would be in the mood to listen.

'I did what I thought was right,' said Titch, feeling gloomy as he trudged away, heading for his sleeping quarters. As he turned the corner of the corridor, he bumped into the boy who'd left him to fend off the Wired Bunch alone.

'I thought you were good enough to handle the situation without me,' said Alexei weakly.

'So,' said Titch, 'you slipped back in time for your turn in the simulator, right?'

Alexei looked at the floor. 'Maybe you'll be allowed a session later?' he suggested.

'I doubt that,' Titch said. He was cross with Alexei, but in no mood to hold a grudge. 'If I've missed my chance to join the Championship trail, then so be it. At least I can be proud of my actions.'

•

With training complete, the apprentice pilots no longer had access to the mechs. The machines had been returned to the main hangar, where they stood motionless alongside one another. Unable to sleep that night, Titch slipped out from the bunker and crossed under the moonlight to the hangar. He recognised the mech he'd trained with straight away. It wasn't just the distinctive colours, but the fact that it had suffered more explosion damage than any other.

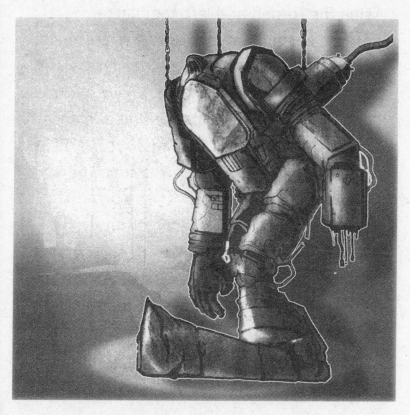

'I just came to say goodbye,' he said, standing between the feet of the towering metal giant. 'I wish we could've had more time together.'

Titch knew the mech was powered down. Even so, he couldn't help but think that inside LoneStar was listening. With a sigh, he turned and left the hangar.

A moment later, two faint traces of red light lit up behind the mech's visor, before fading away once again. At the hangar door, Titch paused and glanced over his shoulder. It was just a silly thought, but he felt sure the machine was aware of his presence.

•

When Graduation Day arrived, nerves were running high among the students. Only Titch had packed his bags, ready to return to life on the cattle ranch with his mum. The only thing that had stopped him from leaving early was his friends. He wanted to support Martha and Finn, and hoped at least that their dreams would come true. Without Martha's engineering skills, and Finn's flair for precision tuning, Titch would never have got the best from his mech in the first place.

It had been a wild ride, from the moment he sneaked into the Academy and throughout the term of hard training that followed. Even if he had messed up his chances of joining the trail, he had high hopes that the twins would pass with flying colours.

Outside, chairs had been laid out beside the runway. Titch sat next to Finn and Martha, just as Marshal Johnson appeared and stood before them at a lectern.

'Before I announce the names of those who have earned their wings,' he began, 'I have a few words to say. Firstly, every single one of you should be congratulated for what you've achieved here. The skills you've gained will serve you well throughout your lives,' he finished, with a glance at Titch.

As the Marshal continued with his speech, Titch's gaze turned to the brand-new, state-of-the-art mech bodies that were lined up on the runway. These were the prizes that each graduate pilot would earn. It was up to them, the engineer and the test pilot what legs, arms and weapons they chose to bolt on. As a team of three, once they set off on the Battle Championship trail, they would be taking part in rounds with very different demands. Whatever the landscape, they needed to make sure their mech was battle-ready.

It was just a shame, Titch thought to himself, that he wouldn't be a part of it.

'Here comes the graduation list,' whispered Martha, which jogged Titch from his thoughts.

He looked up to see Marshal Johnson unroll a sheet of paper.

'The pilots, in no particular order,' he announced, and started reading out the names. Each apprentice he called out practically leapt from their chair with joy. They strode up proudly to shake hands with the Marshal, who handed them a scroll and the key to a mech cockpit.

Then came the engineers and the test pilots. 'Martha and Finn,' he announced, towards the end of the list. 'Very well done to you both.'

The twins punched the air with delight. Titch hugged Martha and shook hands warmly with Finn.

'Best of luck, guys,' he told them.

'Wait!' said the Marshal, and studied the list closely. 'I've missed out a pilot.'

For a moment, Titch held his breath.

'It could be you,' whispered Finn.

The Marshal looked at those who were

left. Then he beamed at one boy in particular.

'Heads up, Alexei! It seems luck is on your side!'

Titch looked around to watch his rival rush to accept a handshake from the Marshal and then a key to his new mech's cockpit. As the round of applause faded out, Titch and those who had failed to earn their wings rose to leave.

'I'm sorry,' said Martha.

'Me too,' added Finn, and glanced at the row of mechs. 'I guess we'll find another pilot to support, but it won't be the same without you.'

Titch smiled bravely. 'I won't forget you guys. You'll make that pilot very proud.' He trudged away, already thinking about what he'd tell his mother, when Marshal Johnson returned to the microphone.

'I also have a special award to hand

out,' he said. When Titch turned around, he found the Marshal was looking directly at him. 'Over the years, I've seen many talented pilots pass through my Academy. Very rarely do I meet one who is exceptional. I'm talking about an individual who isn't just skilled inside a cockpit, but who is prepared to make great sacrifices to save others. It gives me great pleasure to say we have seen one such pilot this term, and he's standing right behind you.'

Everyone turned to see who the Marshal was talking about. Even Titch looked over his shoulder. When he saw that nobody was there, he turned back round and blushed.

'Yay for Titch!' cried Martha.

'You may not have taken part in the simulator test,' the Marshal continued, 'but what you did to save the Academy was outstanding.'

Titch couldn't believe what he was

hearing. He'd thought that the Marshal hadn't approved of what he'd done!

'As a result, I'm pleased to announce that you too have earned your wings.'

Titch just blinked in response. He could barely believe what he'd just heard.

'Me? Really?'

Marshal Johnson held out a set of keys. 'Congratulations, Titch. My security team tell me we'd have been finished without you. It seems I was wrong. They couldn't have dealt with Wyatt and his Wired Bunch alone. Now take these and join the others, before I change my mind.'

Titch's ears filled with the sound of clapping as he approached the Marshal. But as he reached out to accept the keys, something persuaded him to drop his hand once more.

'I know these mech bodies are amazing,' he said nervously looking at the machines behind him, 'but there's really only one machine for me.'

Marshal Johnson looked surprised. Then he followed Titch's eyes as they turned to the hangar. Inside, one of the trainer mechs appeared to have powered up without authorisation. LoneStar! The Marshal looked back at Titch and found him beaming from ear to ear.

'It's a strange request,' he said, looking over at the battered green-and-blue mech, 'and I think you'll find that a beaten-up old model like that will need some customising if it stands any chance at all in the Battle Championship, but if you feel at home inside that cockpit, then go ahead. It's yours!'

'LoneStar and I work well together,' said Titch as he shook hands with the Marshal. 'I'll make sure the mech is fit to fight.'

Overjoyed, Titch ran to join his friends.

'You did it!' cried Finn. 'We all did it!'

'I can't believe we're going to hit the trail together after all!'

'I wish my dad could see this moment,' said Titch, 'I'm doing this for him. With luck, this is my chance to find out what happened.'

'And take part in some fantastic mech fights along the way!' Finn added.

As they spoke, Alexei passed by en-route to inspect his new mech body.

'Congratulations, Alexei,' said Titch, holding out his hand.

Alexei stopped and looked at it disapprovingly. Then he grinned at the three friends. 'We're not apprentices any more. We're qualified Championship contenders! And Championship contenders don't shake hands. Not now we're rivals!'

'OK, then!' said Titch. 'See you on the Championship trail, Alexei. It's going to be quite an adventure. And may the best pilot win!'

'You're looking at him,' replied Alexei. 'Nobody's going to stop me now!'

Titch glanced over his shoulder at the old steel giant in the hangar that he'd just claimed as his graduation prize. A moment later, two lights behind the machine's visor lit up. One then faded out briefly, as if winking at him. When the others turned to see what their friend was smiling at, they saw nothing but a battle-weary mech with no sign of life in it. But Titch knew otherwise.

● ● ●

Check out the next action-packed book in the Battle Champions series. . .

1
Rust Town

Under a blistering sun, Titch and his friend Martha made their way across the plain on horseback. They had been riding throughout the day – a long and tough journey – but finally the end was in sight.

'At last,' Titch declared, pushing back his mop of sandy hair as the old trading post, Rust Town, came into view before them. 'I'm looking forward to a bath and a decent bed for the night.'

'We can't rest straight away.' Martha jabbed a thumb over her shoulder as if to remind Titch of something. 'There's work to be done if we're going to be fighting fit for the first round of the Battle Championship season!'

Titch glanced to where she was pointing and grinned. Close behind them towered a giant mech robot. Every footstep it took caused the ground to shudder. The machine was as high as a house, with two glowing red lights for eyes and a cockpit embedded in its chest. Titch, who was a small boy for his age, craned his neck for a better look. Through the reinforced glass, he could just about see the pilot inside.

'Hey, Finn!' he called, speaking into a microphone clipped to his collar. 'How's it going in there?'

'I'm cool!' came the reply into his earpiece. 'Mostly because Martha fixed the fan unit before we set off!'

Martha chuckled and shook her head. She was a kind-looking girl, with sharp cheekbones and almond-shaped eyes. As the mechanic, it was her job to make sure the mech was fully operational. Her twin brother Finn served as the test pilot, while Titch would take over for the Championship battle rounds. The three friends had only just graduated from Mech Academy, so they were still feeling pretty nervous. Even so, after months of hard training, they were excited about finally having the chance to compete.

'Do you think Alexei will be there yet?' asked Finn over the mech's radio system.

'I hope not,' groaned Titch, thinking about the blond-haired boy who'd graduated with them from Mech Academy. They hadn't exactly hit it off. In fact, they were more like arch-enemies as Alexei was often quick to cheat and even sabotage Titch's chances.

'Let's not think about Alexei now,' said Titch, trying to put the boy out of his mind. 'We've got more important things to worry about,' he added, glancing at the town before them. It stood at the mouth of a huge canyon which looked like a vast and jagged crack in a rocky plain.

'One thing's for sure – you'll have to watch out for attacks from above,' said Martha, her gaze locked on the landscape behind the town. 'That's quite a battle zone!'

Titch could see that for himself. The canyon was enormous! And this weekend, it would host the Battle Championship. Already, grandstands had been erected at the top. At first light tomorrow morning, they would be full of spectators. Then, down below on the canyon floor, the fighting would begin in knockout rounds.

'If I stand any chance of getting through all three rounds,' said Titch, 'I'm going to need eyes in the back of my head!'

'That's where your mech's on-board computer comes in,' chuckled Finn through the headset. 'Remember – the radar screen will stop you from being taken by surprise.

It's your reaction times that matter. If you come under attack and move too slowly, Martha and I can expect to be picking up cogs and gearwheels until sundown.'

Titch smiled at the thought as he steered his horse towards the town. That so wasn't going to happen if he could help it.

He looked about him. Rust Town was a dusty, rough-looking place. Most of the people who came here were just passing through on horseback – from gold hunters to ranch hands. Some of the other Battle Championship competitors had clearly already arrived by the look of the mechs striding down the main street. From a distance, they seemed like giants moving among humans.

Titch watched as one of the mechs stopped outside the town's scavenger store. This was where competitors could pick up parts and weapons for their fighting machines. A set of automatic steps unfolded from the mech's chest. Then the pilot climbed out from the cockpit and made his way inside. Titch hoped the store was well stocked. They had yet to arm their own mech after all.

'First thing we need to do is check in with the officials,' said Martha as they drew their horses to a halt just inside the main gates.

'That's where we need to go.' Titch pointed, drawing their attention to a Battle Championship banner that was strung across the far end of the street. He guided his horse towards it and Martha and Finn followed in a line. Chickens scratched at the dirt in front of them, only to hurry away when they saw the approaching mech. Next they passed the saloon bar. From inside, brooding cowboys stared back at them. Titch tried not to look at them. He and his two friends were much younger than most Championship contenders. They were the new generation of fighters. Titch had proven himself to be bold, brave and lightning quick but just then, he simply felt like a new boy on his first day at school. The last thing he wanted was trouble . . .